LET'S PLAY
SPORTS!

Tennis

by Kieran Downs

BLASTOFF! READERS
2

BELLWETHER MEDIA • MINNEAPOLIS, MN

Blastoff! Readers are carefully developed by literacy experts to build reading stamina and move students toward fluency by combining standards-based content with developmentally appropriate text.

Level 1 provides the most support through repetition of high-frequency words, light text, predictable sentence patterns, and strong visual support.

Level 2 offers early readers a bit more challenge through varied sentences, increased text load, and text-supportive special features.

Level 3 advances early-fluent readers toward fluency through increased text load, less reliance on photos, advancing concepts, longer sentences, and more complex special features.

★ **Blastoff! Universe**

Reading Level

Grade
K

Grades
1–3

Grade
4

This edition first published in 2021 by Bellwether Media, Inc.

No part of this publication may be reproduced in whole or in part without written permission of the publisher. For information regarding permission, write to Bellwether Media, Inc., Attention: Permissions Department, 6012 Blue Circle Drive, Minnetonka, MN 55343.

Library of Congress Cataloging-in-Publication Data

Names: Downs, Kieran, author.
Title: Tennis / by Kieran Downs.
Description: Minneapolis, MN : Bellwether Media, Inc., 2021. | Series: Blastoff! readers: let's play sports! | Includes bibliographical references and index. | Audience: Ages 5-8 | Audience: Grades K-1 | Summary: "Relevant images match informative text in this introduction to tennis. Intended for students in kindergarten through third grade"– Provided by publisher.
Identifiers: LCCN 2019054199 (print) | LCCN 2019054200 (ebook) | ISBN 9781644872185 (library binding) | ISBN 9781618919762 (ebook)
Subjects: LCSH: Tennis–Juvenile literature.
Classification: LCC GV996.5 .D69 2021 (print) | LCC GV996.5 (ebook) | DDC 796.342–dc23
LC record available at https://lccn.loc.gov/2019054199
LC ebook record available at https://lccn.loc.gov/2019054200

Editor: Christina Leaf   Designer: Josh Brink

Printed in the United States of America, North Mankato, MN.

Table of Contents

What Is Tennis?

Tennis is a sport in which players hit a ball across a **court**.

Players compete in **singles** or **doubles**. They score points to win games.

doubles

4

Tennis is played around the world! It is popular in the United States.

- **United States tennis player**
- **singles and doubles**
- **Accomplishments:**
  - **23 Grand Slam singles titles**
  - **14 Grand Slam doubles titles**
  - **4 Olympic gold medals**
  - **9th woman to finish the career Grand Slam**

It is also a favorite in Europe and Australia.

What Are the Rules for Tennis?

serve

Tennis games begin when one player **serves**. This player hits the ball across the net from the **baseline**.

They get a second chance if they do not make it.

baseline

The other player **returns** the serve. The ball must bounce once before a serve is returned.

Then the player must hit it back.

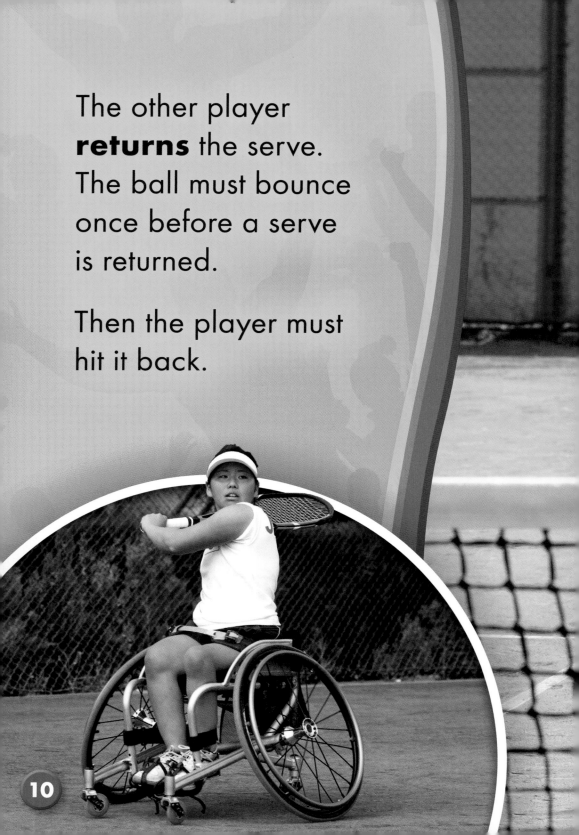

Points are scored when the ball cannot be returned. The ball must land **in bounds** to count as a point.

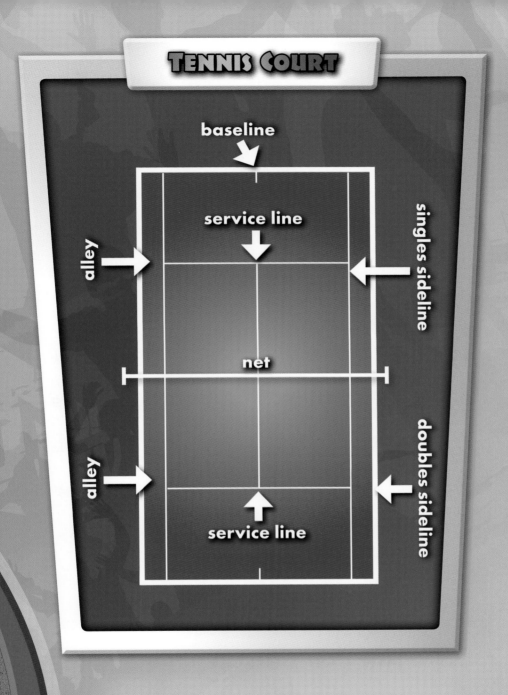

baseline

service line

alley

singles sideline

net

alley

doubles sideline

service line

Doubles **matches** have larger boundaries.

The first person
to score four points
wins a game.

Games usually must be
won by at least two points.

Players must win six games to win a **set**.

Most matches have up to three sets. Whoever wins the most sets wins the match!

racket

visor

Players use **rackets** to hit the ball.

TENNIS GEAR

tennis ball

tennis shoes

visor or hat

racket

Players wear **visors** and hats. This keeps the sun out of their eyes.

Light clothes let players move well. Tennis shoes help them to not slip.

Tennis keeps players on their toes!

Glossary

baseline—the line marking each end of the court

court—the area that tennis is played on

doubles—a tennis match in which players are on teams of two

in bounds—within the boundaries of the court; the sidelines and baseline make up the boundaries of a tennis court.

matches—contests between two or more individuals or teams

rackets—pieces of equipment that have handles, oval frames, and a net of strings that are used to hit tennis balls

returns—hits the ball back to the other player

serves—hits the ball to start play

set—a group of games that count toward deciding a winner; most tennis matches have up to three sets.

singles—a tennis match in which players are by themselves

visors—brims that help keep the sun out of someone's eyes

To Learn More

AT THE LIBRARY

Derr, Aaron. *Tennis: An Introduction to Being a Good Sport*. South Egremont, Mass.: Red Chair Press, 2017.

Meltzer, Brad. *I Am Billie Jean King*. New York, N.Y.: Dial Books for Young Readers, 2019.

Moening, Kate. *Serena Williams: Tennis Star*. Minneapolis, Minn.: Bellwether Media, 2020.

ON THE WEB

FACTSURFER

Factsurfer.com gives you a safe, fun way to find more information.

1. Go to www.factsurfer.com.

2. Enter "tennis" into the search box and click Q.

3. Select your book cover to see a list of related content.

Index

The images in this book are reproduced through the courtesy of: Patrick Foto, front cover (girl); Mark Winfrey, front cover (background); ESB Professional, pp. 4, 16; kali9, p. 5; Marshalik Mikhail, p. 6; Leonard Zhukovsky, p. 7; ptaxa, p. 9; 101akarca, p. 10; pajtica, p. 11; JJ pixs, p. 12; Slatan, p. 14; Statos Giannikos, p. 15; skynesher, p. 17; andresr, pp. 18-19, 21; Ellie.tuang, p. 19 (top left); Solis Images, p. 19 (top right); AboutLife, p. 19 (bottom left); Andrew Ivan, p. 19 (bottom right); didesign021, p. 20; Evegenii Matrosov, p. 23.